PLANET 51

IT CAME FROM PLANET EARTH!

HarperFestival is an
imprint of HarperCollins Publishers.
Planet 51: It Came from Planet Earth!
© 2009 Ilion Animation Studios,
HandMade Films International & A3 Films.
Planet 51™ and all related characters, places, names and other
indicia are trademarks of Ilion Studios, S.L., HandMade Films
International Limited & A3 Films S.L. All Rights Reserved.
Printed in the United States of America.
No part of this book may be used or reproduced in any manner whatsoever
without written permission except in the case of brief quotations embodied
in critical articles and reviews. For information address
HarperCollins Children's Books,
a division of HarperCollins Publishers,
10 East 53rd Street, New York, NY 10022.
www.harpercollinschildrens.com
Library of Congress catalog card number: 2009928951
ISBN 978-0-06-184416-4

Typography by Joe Merkel
09 10 11 12 13 UG 10 9 8 7 6 5 4 3 2
❖
First Edition

PLANET 51

IT CAME FROM PLANET EARTH!

Adapted by
Annie Auerbach

HARPER FESTIVAL
An Imprint of HarperCollinsPublishers

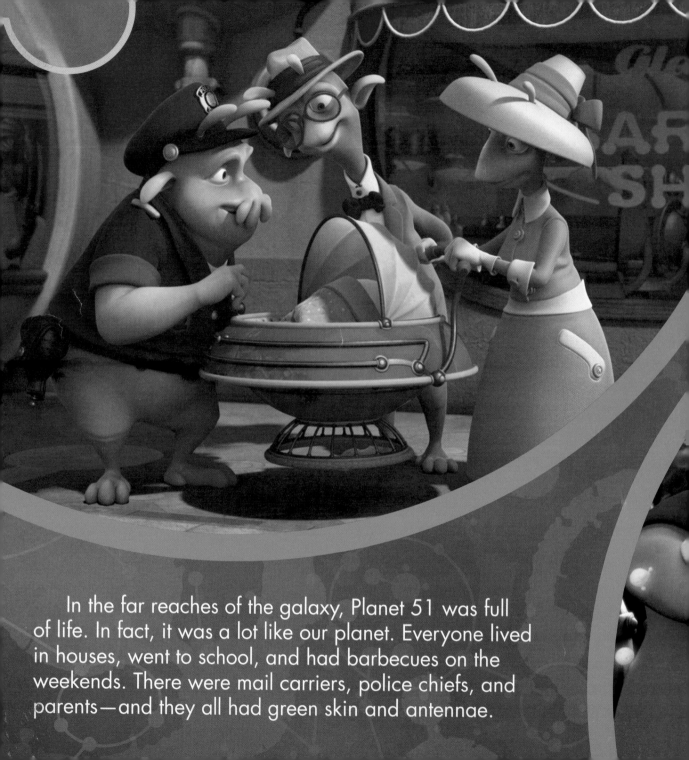

In the far reaches of the galaxy, Planet 51 was full of life. In fact, it was a lot like our planet. Everyone lived in houses, went to school, and had barbecues on the weekends. There were mail carriers, police chiefs, and parents—and they all had green skin and antennae.

Everyone on Planet 51 loved watching movies—especially 3-D ones about aliens. But in these movies, *humans* were the aliens. *The Beast with Ten Fingers* was a huge hit here!

There were even field trips on Planet 51. A popular one was to the planetarium. There, a teenager named Lem presented a show all about the galaxy.

"The only known intelligent life is right here on our planet," Lem told the schoolkids. He said there was no such thing as humans.

He tried not to show that he was a little nervous. If the show went well, Lem would be promoted to junior assistant curator.

A little while later, Lem sprinted out of the planetarium. "You're looking at the new junior assistant curator!" he said proudly.

His friends, Skiff and Eckle, congratulated him.

"High four!" Lem said, holding up his hand.

"High four!" said Skiff, slapping his friend's hand.

The next day, as Lem and Eckle's families were enjoying barbecue, a fiery rocket streaked across the sky. To their horror, the ship landed right in Eckle's backyard! It was clear it was an *alien* ship!

The hatch opened, and a human astronaut stepped out. He planted the American flag, and then took a look around. He realized the planet definitely wasn't deserted. In fact, he was surrounded by little green men!

Lem's family and neighbors were in shock. There was a real live human standing right in front of them! They were too scared to even scream.

Suddenly Eckle realized that the spaceman was like the kind in his beloved comic books. Eckle tried to get an autograph, but that just seemed to scare the astronaut.

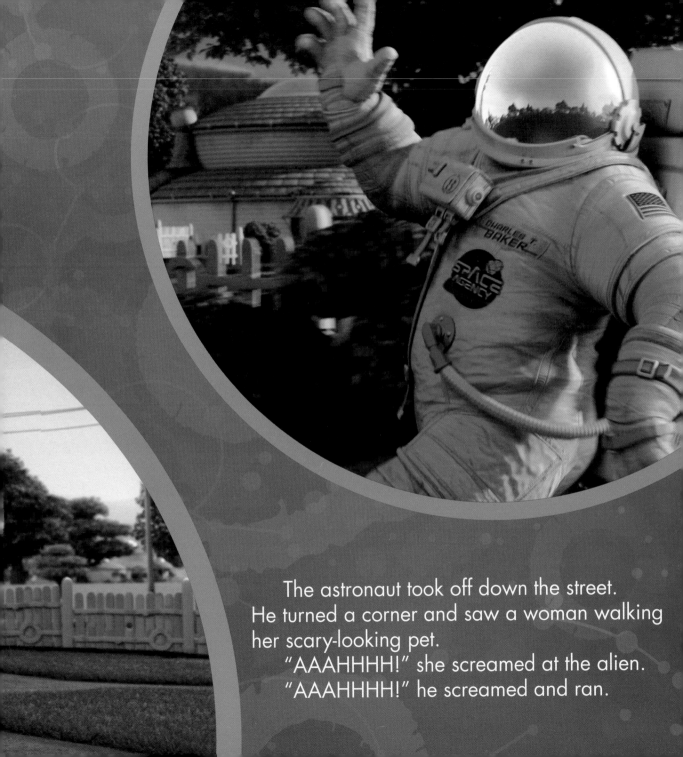

The astronaut took off down the street.
He turned a corner and saw a woman walking
her scary-looking pet.
"AAAHHHH!" she screamed at the alien.
"AAAHHHH!" he screamed and ran.

That evening, the newscast reported that there had been several sightings of the strange human from another planet. The army was preparing for battle, and residents were urged to call the alien hotline if they spotted the invader.

"Our very survival depends on it," the newscaster told the viewers.

The next day, Lem went to work at the planetarium. He tried to concentrate on his job but often found himself thinking about the alien that had landed.

When he was closing up for the day, he made a big discovery: the alien sleeping among the exhibits!

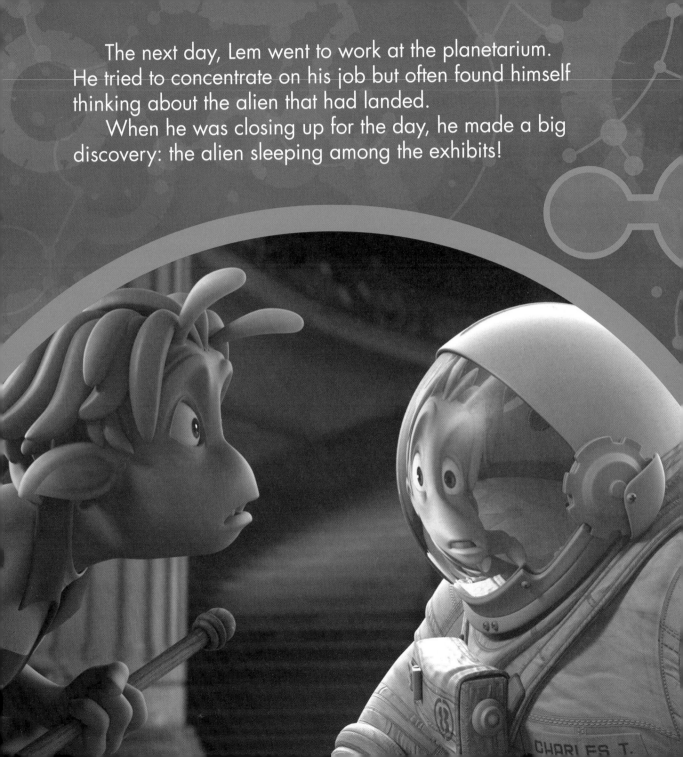

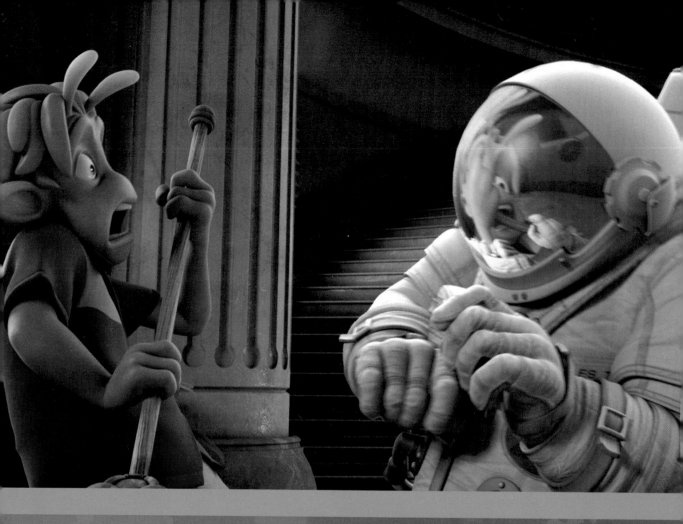

Then the astronaut woke . . . and he and Lem both screamed and ran away. But the planetarium was round, and they ran right into each other! Once again, they turned and fled in opposite directions.

Lem dashed to the nearest phone and dialed.

"Hello . . . ," said a voice on the line.

"Yes, hi!" exclaimed Lem. "I found the alien."

"Due to a high call volume, we will be with you as soon as we can," the voice said.

Lem rolled his eyes. "You've got to be kidding." He had the alien in his sight and was on hold!

The astronaut was also having a little problem. Actually, it was quite a big problem. One of the hoses on his space suit had become caught and pulled out.

His oxygen was quickly draining, and he was in trouble. With no other choice, the astronaut pulled off his helmet, holding his breath. Would this be the end for him?

Finally the astronaut let out a breath and took in another. "I can breathe!" he cried gleefully.

"You speak my language," Lem said to him with a puzzled look on his face.

"That's amazing! You speak *my* language!" said the astronaut. "I'm Captain Charles T. Baker. Chuck."

Lem introduced himself and then asked, "Are you here to take over our world . . . and eat our brains?"

"Whoa, hold on!" said Chuck. "What kind of sick alien planet is this?"

"Hey, I'm not the alien here, you are," Lem said.

Chuck's eyebrows furrowed. "No, *you* are."

This argument went on for a while. . . .

COUNTDOWN
74:21:48

At last, Chuck said, "Look, there's a command module in orbit right now. It has to leave in seventy-four hours, or it runs out of fuel. If I'm not on it, it goes back to Earth without me. I have to get back to my ship and go back up in space. Can you help me?"

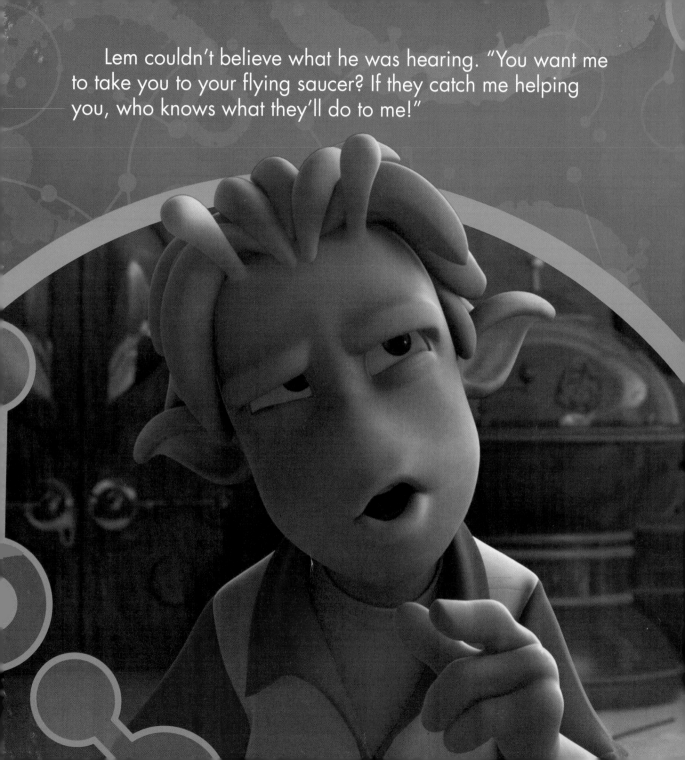

Lem couldn't believe what he was hearing. "You want me to take you to your flying saucer? If they catch me helping you, who knows what they'll do to me!"

Chuck locked eyes with Lem. "Kid, you're my only hope."
Lem blinked. An alien was begging for his help.
Perhaps this alien isn't dangerous after all, Lem thought.

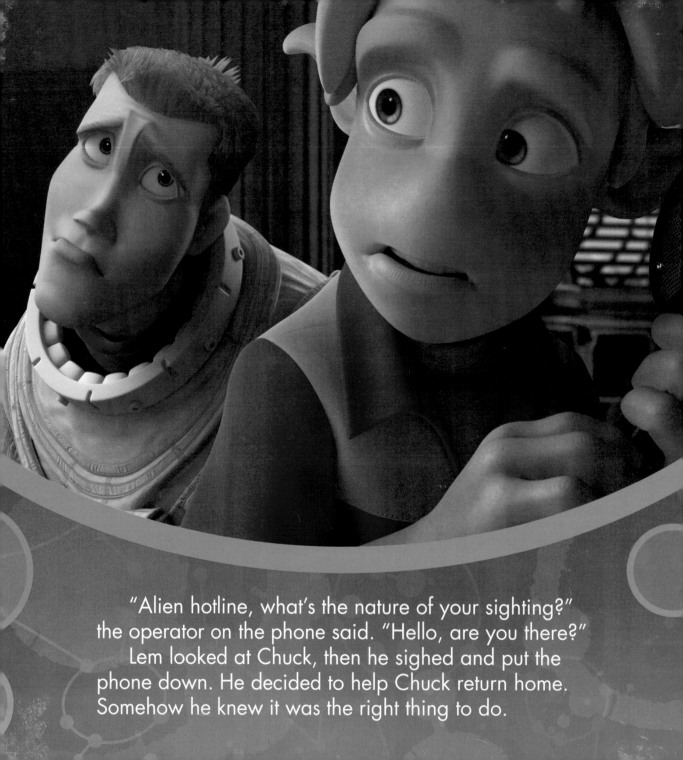

"Alien hotline, what's the nature of your sighting?"
the operator on the phone said. "Hello, are you there?"
Lem looked at Chuck, then he sighed and put the
phone down. He decided to help Chuck return home.
Somehow he knew it was the right thing to do.